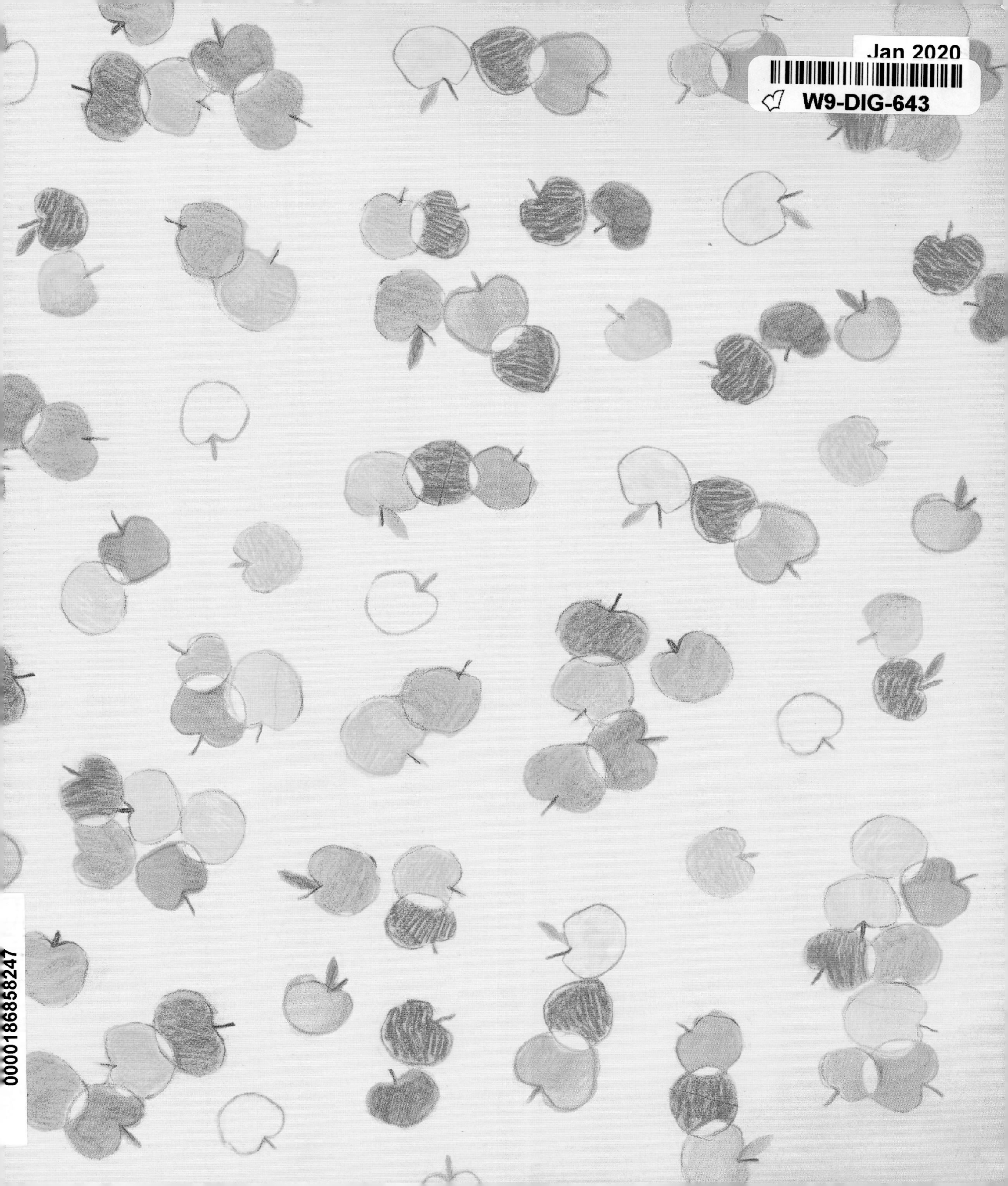

For my children and 'the cousins' — Gus, Maxi, Penny, Tom, Peggy and Martha — all of whom have seen the bright green door at the very top of the old fruit shed and wondered...—KK

To Sofia—LM

Little Hare Books
an imprint of
Hardie Grant Egmont
Ground Floor, Building 1, 658 Church Street
Richmond, Victoria 3121, Australia

www.littleharebooks.com

First published 2017

Cataloguing-in-Publication details are available from the National Library of Australia

978 1 760124 91 5 (hbk.)

Edited by Margrete Lamond and Alyson O'Brien
Production management by Sally Davis
Designed by Vida & Luke Kelly
Produced by Pica Digital, Singapore
Printed through Asia Pacific Offset
Printed in Shenzhen, Guangdong Province, China

5 4 3 2 1

The illustrations in this book were created with ink and pencils on thick watercolour paper.

By Kim Kane
Illustrated by Lucia Masciullo

ENOUGH APPLES

LITTLE HARE
www.littleharebooks.com

At the very top of the fruit shed,
behind a bright green door,
on Old Uplands Farm, lived a tiny man
who loved apple pie.

The sweet smell reminded him
of laden trees and tables.

The scalloped edges reminded him
of family thumbs all pressing into
thick buttery dough.

The tiny man grew his apples
in a higgledy-piggledy orchard
with soil as rich as chocolate.

His eye was keen for spotting bruises,
his arms were long for plucking fruit
from the very top branches and
his toes were splayed for climbing.

He grew apples that smelt tart
and tasted sweet and clear.

One afternoon, New-Build Ned
knocked on the bright green door.

New-Build Ned wore a sturdy yellow hat.

'Will you sell me your land, tiny man?' asked New-Build Ned.

The tiny man shook his head. 'Without land
I'll have no apples and without apples I'll have no pie.'

As the tiny man's apples ripened, farms beyond his fence were taken over by New-Build Ned, who sliced up the land like birthday cake.

Ned dug. Ned poured. Ned shunted.

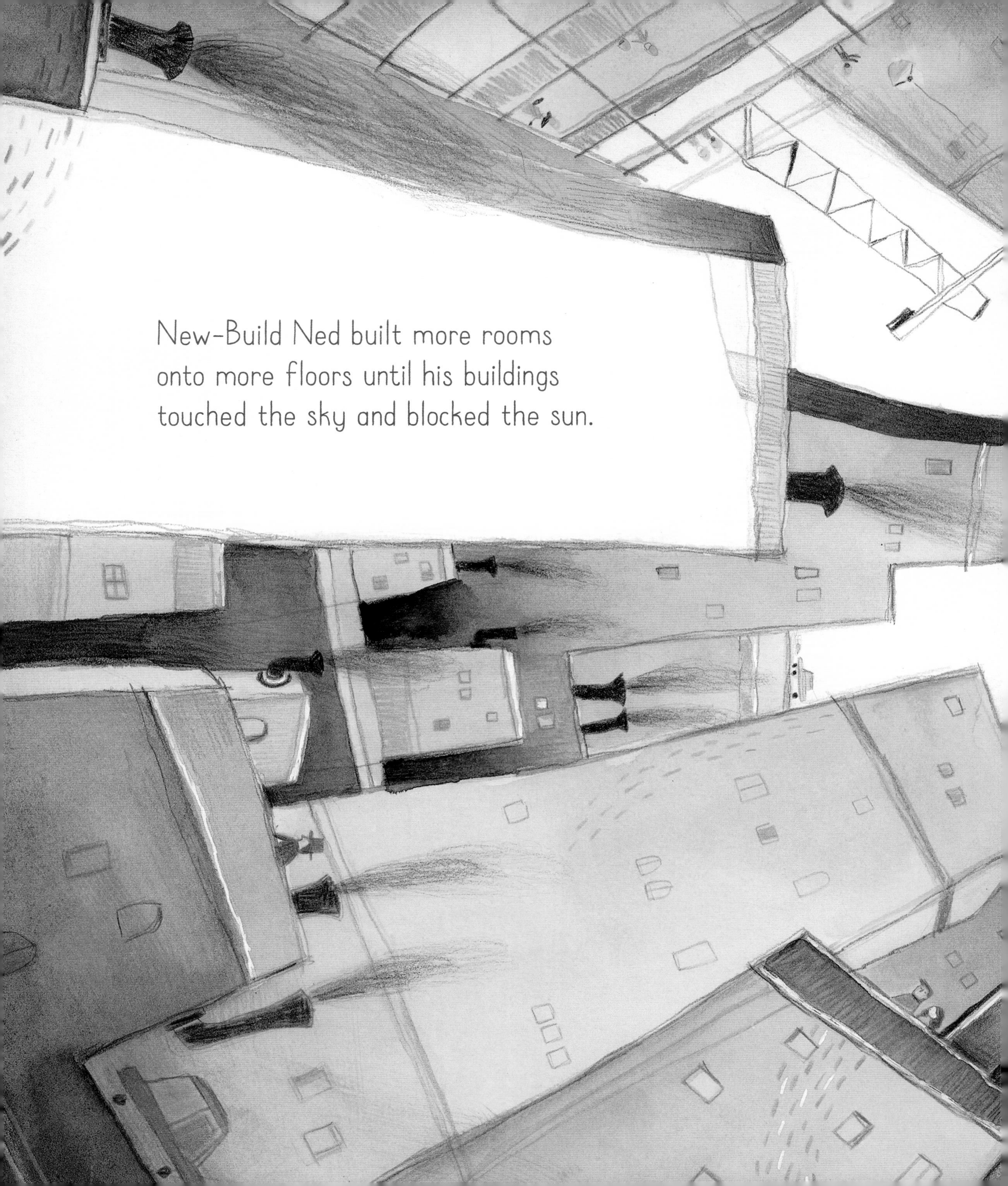

New-Build Ned built more rooms
onto more floors until his buildings
touched the sky and blocked the sun.

The tiny man's orchard
grew danker and dimmer.
He put up mirrors
to catch the sun.

But his apples grew soft in the shadows,
his soil became as pale and as stiff as old porridge
and his apples no longer smelt so tart
nor tasted so sweet.

'This is no way to grow apples,'
thought the tiny man.

One afternoon, the tiny man sniffed at his pie.
It didn't smell like anything much at all.

'What can I do?' he wondered. 'Apples need water and sunlight and clean crisp air. Without good apples there can be no pie.'

In the morning, the tiny man went looking for water and sunlight and clean crisp air.

He found a little here
and a little there.

Up high.

Down low.

Around corners.

And across walls.

In pots and pans and puddles.

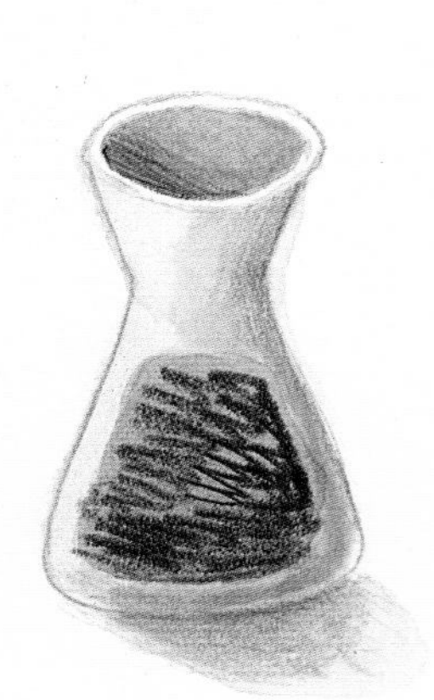

And wherever he found some, he pressed a seed higgledy-piggledy into a handful of soil.

At the very top of a shop,
above a busy street,
behind a bright green door,
lives a tiny man.

Downstairs, he sells the apples
that he helps people to grow ...

Up high.

Down low.

Around corners.

And across walls.

In pots and pans and puddles.

The tiny man's eye is still keen
for spotting bruises,
his arms are still long for plucking fruit
from the very top branches,
his toes are still splayed for climbing ...